Bitter the wind tonight,
combing the sea's hair white...
no need to fear
the proud, sea-coursing warrior.

—Ninth-Century monk

For Arthur

scriptionibus potens

EMILY ARNOLD McCULLY

THE PIRATE QUEEN

G. P. PUTNAM'S SONS

LONG AGO, when Ireland was all untamed, the greatest captain and pirate of the age sailed forth from Connaught in the west. Grania O'Malley was her name.

For centuries O'Malleys pulled lobster, herring, and salmon from the coiling seas. Their cattle dotted the meadows ashore. Most sailors were pirates if they got the chance, and O'Malleys were no different.

When the clan elected Owen O'Malley their chief, he was a wealthy man. His daughter was born at their Clare Island castle in 1530. Owen lifted the infant in his arms and his wife remarked, "Look, she has the light of the sea in her eye."

The friars taught Grania to read Latin sitting beneath the O'Malley motto, *Terra Mariq Potens* — Invincible on Land and Sea. As soon as she could tie a knot, Grania begged to sail with the fleet. Her mother said it was no life for a young girl, but Grania wouldn't give up. She ran off and returned with her hair shorn like a boy's. Her parents laughed at her willfulness and nicknamed her Grania the Bald. She had won the right to go to sea.

Owen taught Grania the ways of the lashing tides and the siren winds. Soon every cranny along the coast was familiar, and she was at home on the black deep. When the horizon was empty of ships, Grania could outdance the nimblest sailor and outgamble him too.

Over the years, Grania grew lithe and strong. One day as the fleet sailed
home with a load of fine Spanish cloth and gold, an English vessel swooped
down on them. "Turn about!" Owen cried, but it was too late. The English
pirates streamed onto the lead O'Malley ship.

Grania's father had told her to hide below if there were a battle, but the
way was blocked. Grania leapt to the rigging and scrambled up. She saw

her father stumble across the deck, wounded. Behind him an English pirate raised his dagger. Shrieking an Irish curse, Grania pounced.

The Englishman went down. "It's a maiden!" the pirates cried in awe.

"Aye, and she's ours!" shouted the O'Malley crew. They fought ferociously until the English were captured and in chains.

By the force of her courage, a sea queen was born.

WHEN SHE WAS SIXTEEN, it was time for Grania to marry, as all girls did. She and her parents chose hot-tempered Donal O'Flaherty, of another seafaring clan. Grania was soon in charge of the O'Flaherty fleet. Under her command, ships patrolled the outer islands, extracting a fee for the use of the waters. If a captain refused to pay, she gave the signal and her men removed the cargo. She was as brave as the stoutest of her followers and they loved her for that.

Grania's first son was born on the high seas. She named him Owen, after her father. When Turkish pirates attacked her galley the next day, the mate scurried down to fetch her.

"What?" She laughed. "You can't do without me for a single day?"

She exchanged the babe for a blunderbuss, put it under her cape, and burst onto the deck. There she danced a wild jig, freezing the Turks in their tracks. Grania whipped out her blunderbuss and fired it off. The Turks dove over the gunwales.

Grania loved this life, hard as it was.

Throughout their marriage, Donal fought brawls until he met his end at the hands of a rival clan. Grania was entitled to a widow's portion of his property, but the O'Flahertys refused to give it to her. So Grania hired a new crew, consisting of men who loved cards and dice as much as she did. "Grania of the Gamblers," many called her.

They established a base at Clare Island, her childhood home. There, piece by piece, she built her sea kingdom.

When Grania had five castles, she controlled all but the northeast side of Clew Bay. There stood stout Rockfleet Castle with its inland harbor. Grania had her eye on it, too. From Rockfleet she would be able to see any ship that entered the bay. To its safety she could scurry from attackers on the open sea. The more she considered Rockfleet, the more she had to have it. She thought of a way.

Doona Castle

ACHILL ISLAND

Kildawnet Castle

Clew Bay Castle

CLARE ISLAND

Carrowmore Castle

INISHBOFIN

Rockfleet Castle

Murrisk Castle

Rockfleet belonged to Richard Burke, known as Richard-in-Iron. One day Grania strode up to his door and said, "Let us marry. We two can withstand any invasion the English may send." Richard-in-Iron was delighted to accept Grania's proposal. The sixth and finest castle was now hers.

But Richard, like Donal before him, proved more hotheaded than shrewd. He mounted a rebellion against the duke of Desmond. Grania had no quarrel with the duke, but she went along for Richard's sake. Everyone who saw her in action was awestruck. She flew into the thick of battle, knocking knights off their steeds. But in the end she was outnumbered and the duke captured her.

Never before confined by anyone, Grania was thrown into prison in Limerick. The dungeon was miserable and she longed to be free, but her spirit never faltered. After a year and a half, the Lord Justice in Dublin unexpectedly sent for her.

"I will release you, Grania O'Malley," he said, "but you must promise to end your career of pirating and marauding."

What could she say? Grania said she would. Her heart knew otherwise.

She returned to Connaught, determined to be a pirate again. Richard-in-Iron had died a natural death while Grania was in prison. Now she would reside alone at Rockfleet.

Bᴜᴛ ɪɴ Lᴏɴᴅᴏɴ, Queen Elizabeth I dispatched a ruthless new governor, Sir Richard Bingham, to subdue the Irish. He hanged or massacred all who resisted the new English laws. Bingham had heard of the famous woman pirate and was determined to destroy her. He began by sending his forces to find her son, Owen.

Owen innocently offered the soldiers hospitality, but they accused him of hiding rebels, tied him up, and murdered him. Then they made off with his herd of cattle.

Grania wept bitterly, but before she could plot her revenge, a strange letter arrived from Sir Richard Bingham himself. Given the unrest, he wrote, she must come and live under his protection.

She hadn't the power to make war on the English governor. It seemed there was no choice but to go as Sir Richard ordered. Grania set forth with her men and herds. Before two days were out, they were ambushed by none other than Sir Richard's soldiers. His safe passage was a lie! Her cattle and mares were stolen, her followers scattered. The pirate queen was tied up like an animal.

When she was brought to Sir Richard, he pointed to a gallows. "I've had this made just for you, Grania O'Malley," he said. "You'll die tomorrow."

But that evening a powerful Irish lord rode up and asked that Grania be spared. "I give my word," he said. "She will never be pirate nor rebel again."

Sir Richard gave her a sneering glance. "Why not spare you?" he mused. "There's nothing left of you, Grania O'Malley. Your men, your herds, your castles are gone. From what I hear, your ships are all broken as well. Go back to Clew Bay."

Grania hastened to see if Bingham had uttered the truth this time. She found a sorry scene. Her fleet had been broken in a storm, Clew Bay and Galway were controlled by English ships. Her sea kingdom was no more. Only the Clare Island castle was hers.

On the great cliffs that had been the seat of her power, the old sea queen pondered. After decades of fighting, her enemy Bingham now was the most powerful man in Ireland. What's more, his tactics were vicious and cruel. But who sat above Bingham, with greater might even than his? Another woman warrior—the queen of England!

Grania would demand justice of Elizabeth I.

So Grania O'Malley decided to go to London and see the queen in person. Her loyal followers begged her not to go. No Irish chieftain had dared set foot on English soil. Nothing in Elizabeth's reign vexed her more than the Irish. And when vexed, she had been known to scold people, slap them, and cut off their heads.

When Grania was brought before the queen, she stated her case in Latin, the only language they shared.

Elizabeth asked how the troubles in Ireland might be ended. "Sir Richard Bingham's brutality makes the people rebel all the more," Grania replied. Elizabeth frowned, and whispered to one of her advisors.

Grania offered to "harry the queen's enemies with fire and sword on land and sea." If Elizabeth accepted her offer, Grania would be back in business—and Sir Richard could do nothing about it.

Then Grania sneezed.

A lady-in-waiting handed her a handkerchief of embroidered cambric lace. Grania blew noisily.

"Oh!" the courtiers gasped as she tossed it into the fireplace.

The queen's hard eyes flashed. "Is this what you think of our fine English cloth?" she said. "It was meant for your pocket."

"What?" said Grania, astonished. "In Ireland we value cleanliness more than to put a soiled thing in our pocket." A terrible silence followed. The queen frowned darkly. Everyone waited to hear her pronounce the death sentence on the rude Irish pirate. Elizabeth's mouth twitched. She laughed. After a startled moment, the courtiers laughed. Grania laughed. The great chamber rocked with mirth.

"Your customs may be strange," the queen declared, "but you have led your people bravely. I accept your offer to defend the Crown with fire and sword. Also I grant you maintenance from your husbands' lands."

She had won! Grania made a bow of thanks and the court applauded. The meeting of queens was over.

Grania returned to Ireland, fitted up a fleet, and was soon a pirate again. Bingham did his best to ruin her, but she was more than his match. Grania O'Malley died, for all we know, at the helm of a galley, in the thick of a fight.

AUTHOR'S NOTE

What we know of Grania—Granuaile, in Old Irish, or Grace, in English—O'Malley comes from a few contemporary documents and voluminous legends. When Grania petitioned Elizabeth I, Lord Burghley, the Queen's counselor, responded with eighteen questions. Grania's answers tell of her parentage, marriages, and late suffering at the hands of Sir Richard Bingham. Beyond these facts lie extravagant myths that naturally attached to so fierce and colorful a figure. They turn up in various places, among them an antique review of the Galway Archeological Society, travel writings, folklore collections, and Anne Chamber's excellent biography, published in Ireland. I have selected and simplified episodes that could be contained within a picture book.

Apparently, Grania had a half brother, but she may have been raised as an only child—certainly as her father's heir. She had three children by Donal O'Flaherty and one by Richard Burke (a.k.a. Richard-in-Iron). When she appeared before Sir Henry Sidney, the English deputy, with three galleys, two hundred fighting men, and her husband Richard, to offer her services, he noted that "she was as well by sea as by land, well more than Mrs. Mate with him," referring to Richard. But when it suited her purposes to fight the English, she did. She sided with the power of the moment, English or Irish, as long as it furthered her own purpose.

Insurrection and repression marked all the years of Grania's life. Henry VIII had begun a policy of "Submit and Regrant," which encouraged Irish chieftains to turn over their lands to the Crown's jurisdiction in return for an English title. Elizabeth continued it.

In spite of the turbulence in Ireland, Grania strove to protect her independence, scheming for "maintenance by land and sea." Her skill as a sea captain, her courage, and her cunning allowed her to survive an era of war, intrigue, imperialism, and lawlessness, filled with larger-than-life men and women. The meeting of the Pirate Queen and the Virgin Queen was not one of equals, but a confronting of ruler by rebel. Fearless Grania would truly stop at nothing to pursue her calling!

E.A.McC.

Copyright © 1995 by Emily Arnold McCully · All rights reserved. This book, or parts thereof, may not be reproduced in any form without permission in writing from the publisher. · G. P. Putnam's Sons, a division of The Putnam & Grosset Group, 200 Madison Avenue, New York, NY 10016 · G. P. Putnam's Sons, Reg. U.S. Pat. & Tm. Off. · Published simultaneously in Canada. Printed in Singapore. Book design by Cecilia Yung. Lettering by David Gatti. Text set in Cochin. Library of Congress Cataloging-in-Publication Data McCully, Emily Arnold. The pirate queen / written and illustrated by Emily Arnold McCully. p. cm. 1. O'Malley, Grace, 1530?–1603?—Juvenile literature. 2. Ireland—History—1558–1603—Biography—Juvenile literature. 3. Women pirates—Ireland—Biography—Juvenile literature. [1. O'Malley, Grace, 1530?–1603? 2. Pirates. 3. Ireland—History—1558–1603. 4. Women—Biography.] I. Title. DA936.043M37 1996 941.505′092—dc20 [B] 94-5389 CIP AC ISBN 0-399-22657-5 3 5 7 9 10 8 6 4 2